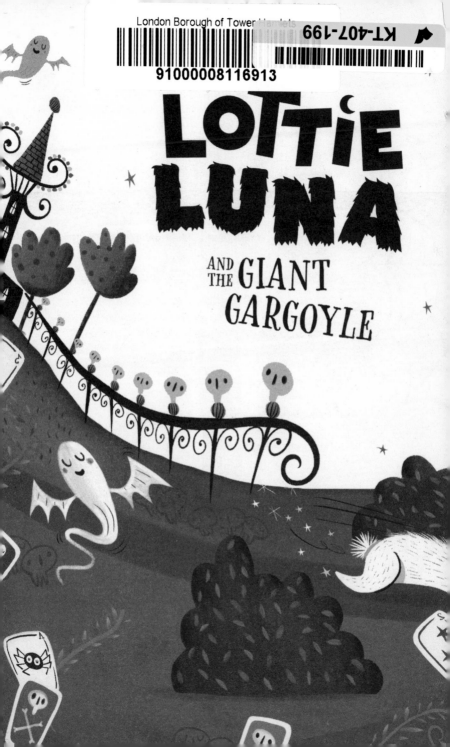

LOTTIE LUNA

AND THE GIANT GARGOYLE

First published in Great Britain
by HarperCollins *Children's Books* in 2021
HarperCollins *Children's Books* is a division of HarperCollins*Publishers* Ltd,
1 London Bridge Street
London SE1 9GF

www.harpercollins.co.uk

HarperCollins*Publishers*
1st Floor, Watermarque Building, Ringsend Road
Dublin 4, Ireland

2

ISBN 978-0-00-834307-1

A CIP catalogue record for this title is available from the British Library.

Printed and bound in England by CPI Group (UK) Ltd, Croydon CR0 4YY

MIX
Paper from
responsible sources
FSC™ C007454

This book is produced from independently certified FSC™ paper
to ensure responsible forest management.

For more information visit: www.harpercollins.co.uk/green

LOTTIE LUNA

AND THE GIANT GARGOYLE

VIVIAN FRENCH

Illustrated by Nathan Reed

HarperCollins *Children's Books*

Lottie Luna books by Vivian French
in reading order

LOTTIE LUNA AND THE BLOOM GARDEN

LOTTIE LUNA AND THE TWILIGHT PARTY

LOTTIE LUNA AND THE FANG FAIRY

LOTTIE LUNA AND THE GIANT GARGOYLE

ABOUT THE AUTHOR

VIVIAN FRENCH is the author of more than 300 books. In 2016 she was awarded an MBE for her services to literature, literacy, illustration and the arts, and in 2018 she received the Scottish Book Trust's Outstanding Achievement Award. She is the co-founder of the critically acclaimed Picture Hooks scheme to help emerging art graduates find their feet in the world of book illustration.

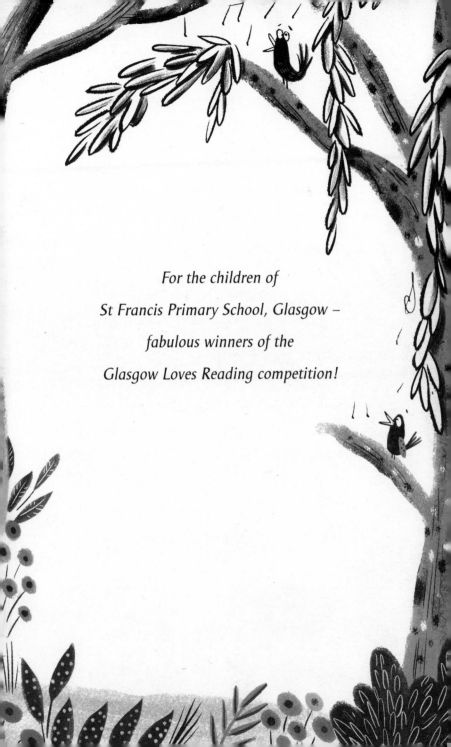

For the children of

St Francis Primary School, Glasgow –

fabulous winners of the

Glasgow Loves Reading competition!

CHAPTER ONE

'**Good** morning, good morning, good morning, darling Ma!' Lottie Luna bounced into the breakfast room, and flung her arms round her mother. Queen Mila, who was sprinkling sugar on her breakfast porridge, looked at Lottie in surprise.

'That's very nice of you, dear. Erm . . . is there any special reason why you're so cheerful?'

Lottie dropped her school bag on the floor, and sat down. 'I'm happy, that's all. It's a Monday, and it's a school day – and I LOVE going to school!'

Boris, Lottie's older brother, snorted. 'Oh yeah? I suppose everyone makes a fuss of you just because you're a princess. But I'll tell you something, Lottie – if you were an ordinary kid, nobody would take any notice of you at all!'

'That's so not true!' Lottie jumped to her feet, her cheeks pink with anger, but before she could say anything more Queen Mila interrupted.

'That's a very unkind thing to say, Boris.' The

queen put a large bowl of porridge in front of him. 'Lottie has a lovely personality . . . she'd make friends anywhere. Lottie, dear – did you want porridge, or toast?'

'Toast, please.' Lottie took a deep breath, and sat down again. Her knees felt wobbly because she had so nearly told her brother the truth – that only her very best friends at school knew she was a princess. All

her other classmates thought she was as ordinary as they were . . . and that was exactly the way Lottie wanted it to be. She made a face at Boris, and rescued the butter from underneath her father's newspaper. King Lupo grunted, and went on reading.

'Some day we must come and see this wonderful school of yours, Lottie,' Queen Mila said as she settled down to her own breakfast. 'Will there be an end-of-term concert, do you think?'

Lottie blinked. It had never occurred to her that there might be such a thing, and she hoped very much that there never would be. If there was, how could she keep the fact that she was a princess a secret? 'I don't think so,' she said. 'Nobody's ever mentioned one.'

Boris snorted again. 'Well, if there is, don't expect me to come.'

4

'You wouldn't be asked,' Lottie snapped back, and she ate the rest of her toast as quickly as she could before picking up her school bag and heading for the door.

'Bye, Ma! Bye, Pa!' And, with a final glare at her brother, she hurried out, followed by Jaws, her pet bat.

Still cross with her brother, Lottie ran as fast as she could along the path, Jaws flying above her. As she came hurtling out of the woods and on to the path that led to Shadow Academy, she saw her two best friends were waiting for her by the gates. Wilf and Marjory were waving madly, and Lottie ran even faster.

'Woweeee!' Wilf said as Lottie skidded to a halt beside them. 'I've never, ever seen you go as fast

as that . . . and I've seen you run loads of times!'

Lottie grinned. She had been born when a lunar eclipse coincided with a full moon, and as a result she had been gifted with extraordinary strength, amazing eyesight and incredibly acute hearing. All Lottie wanted, however, was to be thought of as an ordinary little girl, so she kept her powers hidden

. . . just as she hid her special moonstone necklace. It had been given to her when she was born; when Lottie was happy, her necklace shone as brightly as the moon, but if she was sad or bored or unhappy the necklace was dull and grey.

Lottie's necklace was shining now as she greeted her friends with enthusiastic hugs.

'What's going on?' she asked. 'You look ever so excited!'

'We are!' Marjory gave a little skip. 'Wilf and I met Mrs Wilkolak on the way to school, and she told us a secret . . . Well, it's not really a secret. She'll tell everybody when we get to class, but we know already. Can you guess what it is?'

Lottie thought hard. 'An end-of-term party?'

Wilf shook his head. 'Much better than that!

Lottie . . . there's going to be an end-of-term talent show!'

'There's a talent show for all the juniors every year, but this year it's going to be different – it'll be a competition!' Marjory was bubbling with enthusiasm. 'There's a trophy for the winner – a giant silver gargoyle! Oh, Lottie! Just imagine winning in front of all the mothers and fathers and uncles and grans and everyone! Wouldn't it be completely wonderful!'

A cold hand clutched at Lottie's stomach. 'So . . . are families expected to come and watch?'

Marjory nodded. 'The head teacher sends everyone a personal invitation. It looks ever so grand. Last year my mum had it on the mantelpiece for weeks!'

'My gran did that too,' Wilf said – and then he

paused, and his eyes grew very wide. 'Oh, Lottie! I'm such an idiot! I completely forgot about your parents. The whole school's going to find out that you're a princess! What on earth will you do?'

Lottie shook her head. 'I don't know.' She sounded so miserable that Marjory rushed forward and hugged her.

'We'll help,' she promised. 'If we think hard enough, I'm sure we can come up with something!'

'Thank you,' Lottie said, but she didn't feel convinced.

CHAPTER TWO

Wilf and Marjory tried hard to think of an idea to help Lottie as they walked along the corridor to their classroom, but nothing seemed very practical. 'I'll just have to pretend to be ill on the day of the competition,' Lottie said gloomily.

'That wouldn't be any fun at all,' Wilf told her. 'You absolutely have to see Marjory and me perform our magic act! We're going to be amazing! We tried to do magic tricks last year, but we didn't win because our white rabbit ran away and got stuck under the stage.'

'I didn't know you were good at magic,' Lottie said, and Wilf grinned at her.

'We aren't. Well . . . not very. But we've got over a week to practise. Why don't you join us? We can be the Three Incredibles . . . It'd be brilliant!'

'And we're dying to know what Awful Aggie is going to do,' Marjory added. 'Last year she read a dreadfully boring story, and it went on so long that Mrs Wilkolak fell asleep, and she actually snored! You can't miss it!'

'It does sound huge fun,' Lottie said wistfully. 'If Ma and Pa weren't there, I'd love it.'

Marjory squeezed her arm. 'Don't worry. We've got lots of time to come up with a plan.'

Lottie nodded, but her smile wasn't as sunny as usual. Marjory looked at her anxiously, but before she could say anything Mrs Wilkolak came bustling into the classroom.

'Good morning, everyone!' she said. 'Now – I've something wonderful to tell you! I wonder if anyone can guess what it is?' She winked at Wilf and Marjory. 'Not a word from you two!'

Wilf and Marjory grinned at each other as hands shot up all around them.

'It's a half-day holiday, Mrs Wilkolak!'

'We don't have any homework?'

'There's extra pudding at lunchtime!'

'You're all wrong.' Mrs Wilkolak sounded delighted. 'We've moved the school talent show to the end of this term . . . and for the first time ever it's going to be a competition. There's a very special trophy for the winner!'

Agatha Claws, the girl that Wilf, Marjory and Lottie called Awful Aggie, sat bolt upright, her eyes shining. 'A competition? With a trophy?'

'That's right, Aggie,' Mrs Wilkolak said. 'I can't wait to see what everybody chooses to do. Have you got any ideas?'

Aggie looked thoughtful. 'I'm very good at poetry. I might write a dramatic poem.'

'That sounds interesting,' Mrs Wilkolak told her. 'Lottie . . . what about you?'

Lottie had been wondering if she could persuade Madam Grubeloff, the head teacher,

not to invite her parents, and the question caught her by surprise. 'Ummmm,' she said. 'I haven't really had time to think . . .'

Aggie gave a disdainful sniff. 'And I thought you were so good at everything, Lottie!'

Mrs Wilkolak frowned. 'Agatha! There's no need for that kind of comment! I'm sure Lottie will think of something splendid. And now, please get your lunar diaries out. It's time we got down to work.'

As Lottie's classmates opened their bags to find their diaries, Lottie looked around. A couple of girls caught her eye and smiled at her, and several of the boys gave her cheerful grins.

They like me, Lottie thought. *They like me because I'm the same as them. If they find out I'm a princess, they'll treat me differently – and I'll never feel comfortable again. I won't ever know if they want to be my friend because I'm me, or just because I'm a princess.*

Her mind was whirling, and she made a decision. She would go and talk to the head teacher at breaktime. Madam Grubeloff was the only member of staff at Shadow Academy who knew that Lottie's father was King Lupo, and her mother Queen Mila. *If I explain that she can't invite them, I'm sure she'll understand*, Lottie told herself. *At least, I'm almost sure she will.*

'Lottie?' Mrs Wilkolak's voice broke across Lottie's thoughts, and she jumped.

'Yes, Mrs Wilkolak?'

'I asked if you agreed with Wilf's answer to the first question?' Mrs Wilkolak sounded irritated.

'I'm so sorry,' Lottie said. 'I . . . I don't know.'

'She's worrying about the competition, because clever Lottie Luna always has to win!' Aggie's whisper was loud enough for everyone to hear and, before she knew what she was doing, Lottie swung round and snapped a reply.

'I was not! I've got much better things to think about!'

'Ooooh!' Aggie rolled her eyes. 'So our Lottie Luna has better things to do than win a trophy!'

'That's quite enough, Agatha!' Mrs Wilkolak sounded cross. 'Lottie! Was Wilf's answer correct or not?'

'I'm sorry – I wasn't listening, Mrs Wilkolak.' Lottie shook her head.

The teacher sighed. 'Really! You'd better spend breaktime learning the lunar charts I gave you for homework. Now – can anyone tell me if Wilf was right? Is there only ever one lunar eclipse a year?'

Aggie jumped to her feet. 'That's wrong! You can have up to five!'

Lottie bit her lip. She knew a great deal about lunar eclipses – probably more than any of her classmates. After all, she'd been born during one. She could have answered the question easily if she hadn't been worrying about the talent show . . . and now she was going to be kept in at break, and she wouldn't be able to see Madam Grubeloff.

Mrs Wilkolak was looking at Aggie disapprovingly. 'I'd much rather you didn't call out, Aggie – but you're right. Wilf . . . I'd like you to join Lottie at breaktime. These eclipses mean a lot to us werewolves; they remind us how the earth and the moon are connected to one another. And a full lunar eclipse is particularly important. There's a tradition that any werewolf cub born then has special powers.'

Aggie looked superior. 'My father says that's an old wives' tale. He says it couldn't possibly be true!'

Wilf caught Lottie's eye, and he gave a loud snort that he quickly turned into a cough. 'Oooops,' he said. Lottie looked away . . . and hoped she wasn't blushing.

'A number of old wives' tales are based in truth, Aggie,' Mrs Wilkolak said. 'Now, please turn back to your diaries . . .'

CHAPTER THREE

The rest of the morning dragged for Lottie. At break she and Wilf sat together, staring at the lunar charts, while Mrs Wilkolak read a book, so they couldn't chat. After break, there was a

lesson in star recognition, and Lottie was paired with Aggie. Aggie insisted that she knew all the answers, and wrote them down even though Lottie knew she was wrong. As a result, they came last . . . and, when Mrs Wilkolak asked what had happened, Aggie blamed Lottie.

'Lottie's no good at stars,' Aggie said smugly. 'I've always known the Great Bear was also called the Giant Tripper . . . but she just wouldn't listen.'

Lottie, who had been trying her hardest not to lose her temper, was unable to stay silent any longer. 'It's the Big Dipper! Not Tripper!'

Aggie sniffed. 'That's exactly what I said!'

'No, it wasn't!' Lottie snapped. 'You said Giant Tripper!'

Wilf, with a very straight face, leaned forward. 'Cue for a song, Aggie. "A giant took a trip to the

moon and stars!"' and the class collapsed into fits of laughter. Aggie went a furious purple, and Lottie sighed. She knew Aggie well and, if there was one thing Aggie hated more than anything else, it was being laughed at. Lottie was trying to think of something to say to calm her down when the lunch bell rang, and the moment was lost.

Once lunch was over, Wilf suggested that the Three Incredibles might begin to think about their act for the talent show, but Lottie shook her head. 'I'm going to find something I can do on my own. I might need to pretend to be ill on the day if my parents are coming, and I don't want to let you down.'

'I once painted myself with red spots to

pretend I had measles,' Wilf told her. 'There was a tree identification test, and I hadn't learned anything about it.'

'What happened?' Lottie asked, and Wilf made a face.

'My gran just laughed, and made me wash them off.'

'I was thinking more of a stomach ache,' Lottie said. 'But now I'm going to try and see Madam Grubeloff. If Ma and Pa aren't invited, I won't need to worry about it and there'll be no problem.'

'Do you want us to come with you?' Marjory asked.

Lottie shook her head. 'Could you wait outside for me? I'd like to know you're there.'

The three friends walked together to Madam

Grubeloff's study. Once they were outside, Lottie took a deep breath. 'Wish me luck,' she said and knocked.

'Come in!' The head teacher's voice was as silvery sweet as always, and Lottie's hopes rose as she opened the door.

Madam Grubeloff was sitting at her desk, and in front of her was a heap of cards, and a box of envelopes. She looked up as Lottie came in, and smiled at her.

'Lottie! What can I do for you?'

Lottie was so busy thinking how she should explain her problem that she almost forgot to curtsey. Her heart had started beating very fast, and her knees felt wobbly as she approached the head teacher's desk and said in a rush, 'Please, Madam Grubeloff . . . I really, REALLY don't want my parents to come to the end-of-term talent show because if they do everyone will know I'm a princess and I'd absolutely hate that!'

'You don't want your parents to come?' Madam Grubeloff sounded puzzled. 'But, Lottie . . . wouldn't you like them to enjoy the end-of-term entertainment? And see what you do? And meet your friends?'

Lottie twisted her fingers together as she tried to think of a way to explain how she was feeling.

'I would, if they weren't royal. But I've had such a lovely time being treated just the same as everyone else . . . I don't want to be known as a princess!'

'So do you think your friends would treat you differently?' Madam Grubeloff looked thoughtful. 'I believe that Wilf and Marjory know your secret already, and you seem very happy with them.'

'Oh, I am!' Lottie's eyes shone. 'They're the best! It's just that . . . well . . . not everyone is quite as lovely as they are . . .'

Lottie's voice faded away. How could she say that she was certain Aggie would want to be the best friend of a princess? And Aggie's friends would be just like her. They'd try to push Wilf and Marjory away, and school would never be the same again.

The head teacher sat back in her chair. 'I think I understand, and to a certain extent you have my sympathy. But this is something you should talk through with your parents.' She leaned forward, picked a card off her desk, and slid it into an envelope before handing it to Lottie. 'Here's the invitation. Have a chat when you give it to them.'

Lottie gulped. What should she say? But, before she could think of an answer, the bell rang for afternoon school, and the head teacher jumped up from her desk.

'Goodness! Is that the time? I'm meant to be teaching the little ones in five minutes! Off you go, Lottie, and don't forget to discuss your problem with your mother and father.'

CHAPTER FOUR

Wilf and Marjory were waiting impatiently outside the head teacher's office. As Lottie came out, they bounced towards her.

'What did she say?' Marjory asked.

Lottie sighed. 'She gave me the invitation, and said I should talk to Ma and Pa.'

'Well . . . you could just not hand it over to them,' Wilf said cheerfully.

Lottie was shocked by the suggestion. 'But what if Madam Grubeloff found out?'

'I don't see how she would.' Wilf scratched his

head. 'When they don't turn up at the talent show, she'll just assume they were busy or something.'

Marjory gave Lottie a sympathetic smile. 'Why don't you at least think about it for a bit?'

'And, in the meantime, you can help us practise our magic act!' Wilf bowed low, then spun round in a circle. 'Ladies and gentlemen! Behold the Two Incredibles! We have such

amazing tricks that you won't believe your eyes! Wonderful Wilf and Marvellous Marjory will dazzle you in every way! And assisting us on this special occasion we have . . . what begins with L? Oh! I know! Legendary Lottie!'

Lottie shoved the invitation into her school bag, and grinned at Wilf. 'I like that!' And the three friends linked arms as they made their way back to class.

To everyone's delight, Mrs Wilkolak ended lessons early. 'You can have five minutes to chat about your act,' she said. 'But please keep the noise down. I know it's all very exciting – but we don't want to disturb the rest of the school!'

Aggie put up her hand. 'I know exactly what I'm going to do, Mrs Wilkolak. I've already started. I read a story about a noble werewolf girl who rescued a little werewolf cub, and I'm writing a poem about it.'

Wilf winked at Marjory and Lottie. 'I can't wait to hear that poem . . . not!'

'To be fair, she does write good poems,' Marjory said, and Lottie nodded in agreement.

'Well, I think they're boring,' Wilf told them, 'although I suppose it might be the dreary way she recites them. But we ought to be thinking about the rabbit-out-of-the-hat trick! Hopper got a bit wild last time. I think the top hat was too small.'

Marjory giggled. 'It absolutely was.' A doubtful expression came over her face. 'Didn't you say he'd got even fatter recently, Wilf?'

'Mmmm.' Wilf pulled at his ear. 'We'll need a

bigger top hat. I wonder where we could find one?'

'My dad might have one,' Lottie said eagerly.
'He's got an enormous head. I'll ask him tonight.'

'Fantastic!' Wilf beamed at her. 'Well done,
Legendary Lottie!'

'Everybody back in their seats!' Mrs Wilkolak
clapped her hands. 'We don't want to be late for
the Evening Howl.'

Lottie hurried back to her place. She loved
the Evening Howl. It was a Shadow Academy
tradition; the whole school met in the Great Hall,
and Madam Grubeloff led them in a wonderful
howl of thanks for the day.

Mrs Wilkolak waited until everyone was
settled, and then she went on. 'For homework, I'd
like you to write three hundred words describing
the act you're going to perform. Think hard about

what you've chosen, and make sure you give your act a snappy title.'

'I'm going to be the Tuneful Trumpeter!' Ava said, and two of the boys announced that they were the Tumbling Twins.

'I already know what I'm going to call my poem,' Aggie said. '"The Heroic Tale of Awesome Agatha".'

Wilf rolled his eyes at Lottie and Marjory. 'Bet Mrs Wilkolak goes to sleep again!'

'No whispering, Wilf!' Mrs Wilkolak frowned at him. 'Now . . . get ready to line up at the door.'

As Lottie and her friends walked down the long corridor to the Great Hall, she was thinking about the competition. Half of her was excited, but the other half was still worrying about her parents.

Did she dare to keep the invitation a secret? It didn't feel right.

I'll decide tonight when I get home, she told herself, and at that moment Madam Grubeloff came sweeping on to the stage, her black-and-silver gown shining under the twinkling lights that hung on every wall.

'Good evening, everybody,' she said. 'I want to say a word about the talent show at the end of this term. Although this year it will be a competition, I want every one of you to enjoy the experience, and not to worry about whether you win or not. It's a wonderful opportunity for you to share your

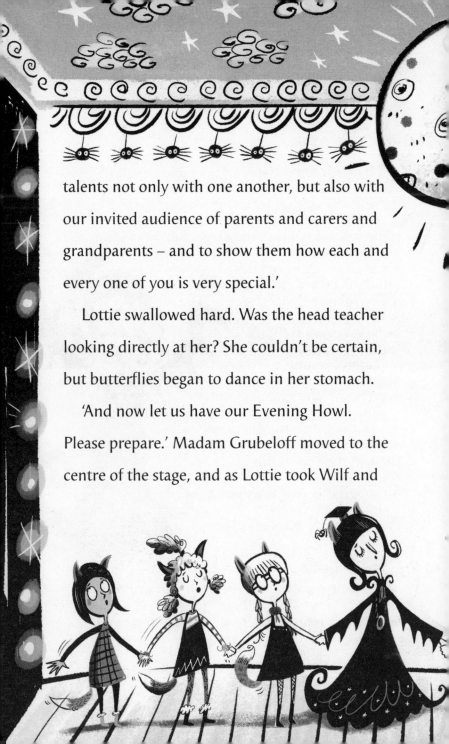

talents not only with one another, but also with our invited audience of parents and carers and grandparents – and to show them how each and every one of you is very special.'

Lottie swallowed hard. Was the head teacher looking directly at her? She couldn't be certain, but butterflies began to dance in her stomach.

'And now let us have our Evening Howl. Please prepare.' Madam Grubeloff moved to the centre of the stage, and as Lottie took Wilf and

Marjory's hands they smiled at each other.

'Wooooooooo!' The head teacher began
the Howl, and one by one the teachers and
students joined in. The sound filled the Great
Hall, and echoed back from the silvery ceiling
where a painted full moon glimmered . . . and
Lottie took a deep breath.

I'm so lucky to be here, she thought. *And I'm
sure everything will turn out all right. It's such a
lovely school, and I have the best friends ever.*

CHAPTER FIVE

As Lottie came dashing through the door to the castle kitchen that evening, she all but crashed into her mother, who was filling a jug of water.

Her brother, who was standing close by, laughed, but Queen Mila sighed. 'I do wish you'd learn not to rush everywhere, Lottie. I nearly dropped the jug!'

'Rush? Rush? Who's rushing?' King Lupo had come in from his office. 'A member of the royal family should always be calm and dignified in every way.'

'Yes, Pa.' Lottie smiled at her father. As she did so, she remembered Wilf's request. 'Pa! I don't suppose you've got a top hat I could borrow? Please?'

'A top hat?' The king looked surprised. 'Have you forgotten that I'm a king, Lottie? A king always wears a crown!'

Queen Mila had been listening. 'I think there might be an old top hat in the attic, Lottie, dear. What did you want it for?'

Lottie suddenly realised she was on dangerous ground. 'Erm . . . it's for Wilf, Ma. He wants to be a magician, and he needs it so he can practise his tricks.'

'Well, your father certainly doesn't need it.' Queen Mila put a huge cheese pie on the table. 'I'll help you to look for it after supper.'

'Thanks, Ma.' Lottie gave her mother a grateful smile, but King Lupo cleared his throat.

'Ahem! I hope that you have no intention of joining in with your friend, Lottie! I would thoroughly disapprove if any daughter of mine was to end up as a magician.'

'Oh, Pa! It's only a bit of fun—' Lottie began,

but her mother gave her a warning glance as she began to serve the pie.

'No arguing at the table,' she said. 'Lottie, dear, why don't you tell us what you did at school today?'

Lottie sighed. 'We worked on our lunar diaries,' she said, and her father immediately launched into a long and boring description of his own school days. As he talked, Lottie ate her cheese pie, thinking about the talent show. Her father's fierce disapproval of magic had shaken her, and by the time she had finished and was helping to clear away the dishes she had made up her mind.

I'm not going to give them the invitation. It's not worth it. What if Pa said something horrid to Wilf and Marjory? I'd feel really terrible. And as soon as supper was over and tidied away Lottie hid the envelope in her bedside cabinet.

That night Lottie didn't sleep very well. Although she'd made up her mind, she was conscious of an uncomfortable feeling in her stomach. Despite his insistence on kingliness, she loved her father dearly, and her mother too.

Just before bedtime the queen had taken Lottie up to the attic, and helped her look through the dusty old chests until they found the top hat.

Queen Mila had even wondered if Wilf needed anything else. 'Has he got a rabbit?' she asked, and when Lottie nodded her mother had given her a huge smile. 'What fun! Maybe he could come to tea one day and show us his tricks? Even if your father's not keen on magic, I'd like to see it.'

Lottie, suffering a terrible pang of guilt, had agreed it would be fun, and the queen handed

her a sparkly green waistcoat. 'Here! I'm sure
Wilf would look like a real magician in this!'

The next day Lottie walked slowly to school,
and she couldn't help noticing that her
moonstone necklace was looking cloudy
and dull. Jaws sat on her shoulder
to comfort her, but even his
encouraging squeaks didn't
cheer her up.

She didn't feel any better when she reached
Shadow Academy. All her classmates were
wildly excited because Madam Grubeloff had
sent out the invitations the night before. One
after another they came bouncing into the
classroom to report how delighted their parents

or grandparents or carers had been when they opened the envelope.

'My gran wants to sit in the front row,' Wilf told Marjory and Lottie.

Marjory nodded. 'My mum's coming too, and all my brothers and sisters. Well . . . not the baby. She's going to stay with a neighbour.'

Mrs Wilkolak smiled. 'That's very thoughtful of your mother. What about you, Lottie? Are your parents coming?'

Lottie found that she was blushing. 'I . . . I'm not quite sure yet,' she said. 'They . . . they're thinking about it.' Much to her relief, she was saved from any further questions by Aggie, who pushed past her to stand in front of the teacher.

'My father and mother are definitely coming,' she announced. 'My father says that when I win

42

he's going to make a special plinth at home for the giant gargoyle trophy. It'll be in the centre of our hall!'

Mrs Wilkolak raised an eyebrow. 'Shouldn't you say IF you win, Aggie?'

'Oh, yes. If I win.' But Aggie didn't sound as if she meant it.

'Everyone sit down, please.' Mrs Wilkolak tapped a ruler on her desk. 'If you work very hard, I might – just might! – let you rehearse this afternoon!'

Lottie was very quiet all morning. At lunchtime, Marjory put an arm round her, and asked, 'Are you okay?'

'I'm fine,' Lottie told her, and then she added,

'I'm just a bit sad that Ma won't see your magic act.'

'So have you decided not to give her and your pa the invitation?' Wilf wanted to know.

'I think so.' Lottie squirmed in her seat. 'I feel mean for not inviting them, but at the same time I really, REALLY don't want them to come and everyone to find out.'

Wilf grinned at her. 'It'll be okay. Madam Grubeloff will never know.'

'Yes . . . but that's making me feel bad too.' Lottie shook her head. 'I'm in a terrible muddle about it all.'

Marjory looked sympathetic. 'There's still time to change your mind.'

'Change your mind about what?' Aggie was taking her lunch tray back to the counter, and

had overheard. 'Hasn't our super-clever Lottie Luna thought of anything yet?' And, with a haughty sniff, she moved away.

Wilf made a face at her back. 'We've absolutely GOT to beat Awful Aggie,' he said, 'even if we don't actually win, Marjory. I brought in all the tricks . . . and Mrs Wilkolak says we can rehearse this afternoon.'

Lottie brightened a little. 'Can I come and watch? I've got the top hat for you – and a sparkly waistcoat!'

Unlike the morning, the afternoon went by in a flash. Wilf was delighted with his waistcoat and insisted on wearing it immediately. 'It's perfect for our magical hankie trick,' he said, and he pulled a yellow handkerchief out of his bag and handed it to Marjory. She showed it to Lottie, and then – 'ABRACADABRA!' Wilf tapped the handkerchief with his wand. Marjory twisted it in between her fingers – and it turned exactly the same green as the waistcoat.

'Wow!' Lottie was genuinely impressed. 'How did you do that?'

Wilf grinned. 'One colour inside the other. It's

our best trick. We sometimes get the others a bit wrong.'

'Look at this one,' Marjory said, and she dived into Wilf's bag and brought out three silver rings, all linked together. She threw them to Wilf, and he waved his wand before dropping them with a crash.

'Oooops!' he said. 'They're meant to separate.' He picked the rings up, and frowned at them. 'They're ever so tricky.'

Five minutes later, the rings still hadn't separated. Wilf was getting more and more frustrated, and even Marjory was getting cross. Trying to calm the situation, Lottie asked, 'What else can you do?'

'I can do a couple of card tricks,' Wilf said,

'and Marjory's really good at mending the cut rope. Much the best bit is the grand finale when Hopper pops out of the hat. I didn't bring him, though.'

Lottie giggled. 'Just as well! Mrs Wilkolak would have gone mad if you had.'

Wilf looked thoughtful. 'That was what went wrong last time . . . but now we've got a decent-sized hat it should be loads easier. I know you're going to do your own act, Lottie, but could you look after Hopper until Marjory and I need him?'

'I'd love to,' Lottie said.

As the bell went for the end of lessons, Mrs Wilkolak tapped on her desk. 'Attention, please! I hope you've all had a useful rehearsal time. Are

there any problems? Anything I can help with?'

Nobody seemed to have any worries, but Aggie put up her hand. 'Please, Mrs Wilkolak – who's going to judge the competition? Will it be someone famous?'

Mrs Wilkolak peered over the top of her spectacles. 'I assume it'll be Madam Grubeloff.'

Aggie looked disappointed. 'Couldn't it be a celebrity? My father's going to bring his camera so he can take pictures.'

'Pictures of her winning, she means,' Wilf whispered to Lottie and Marjory.

Several of the other students had begun to look interested, and Ava called out, 'Why doesn't Madam Grubeloff ask the new king and queen? My mum says the old king came to her school when she was little and handed out the prizes.'

She giggled. 'He got all the names mixed up. He called my mum Snorer instead of Nora!'

That made the whole class laugh, except for Lottie. She was trying hard not to look anxious.

'That's a nice idea, Ava,' Mrs Wilkolak said. 'But I'm sure the royal family are much too busy to judge a school competition.'

'But we could ask, couldn't we?' Aggie was getting more and more excited.

'We'll let Madam Grubeloff decide,' Mrs Wilkolak said firmly, and Aggie was quiet until it was time to go to the Great Hall for the Evening Howl. Taking Ava's hand, Aggie hurried her ahead of the rest of the class, whispering to her as they went. No one else would have known what she was saying, but Lottie's extra-sharp hearing meant she heard every word.

'You know what, Ava? That was SUCH a brilliant idea of yours! Why don't we go and see Madam Grubeloff tomorrow, and ask if the king and queen can judge the competition?'

Before Lottie could hear anything more, the girls had turned the corner of the corridor, and Ava's answer was lost.

Lottie shook her head. It was always difficult when her amazing hearing meant she knew something that other people weren't even aware of – was it unfair to take advantage of her special talents? This time, however, she needed her friends' advice, and she turned to Wilf and Marjory. 'Aggie wants to ask

Madam Grubeloff if Pa and Ma can be the judges!'

Wilf and Marjory stared at Lottie. They knew she could hear things that they couldn't, but even so Marjory couldn't help asking, 'Are you sure?'

Lottie nodded. 'Certain. Oh . . . what am I going to do if Madam Grubeloff says yes?'

Marjory scratched her head. 'Maybe we could go and see Madam Grubeloff too, and say we really want her to be the judge? After all, she's the head teacher, and she knows us.'

'What about a vote?' Wilf suggested. 'If the audience vote, that makes it fairer.'

'That's a much better idea,' Marjory said. 'What do you think, Lottie?'

'It's worth trying,' Lottie agreed. 'Let's go tomorrow morning before lessons start.'

Wilf gave her a high five. 'It's a plan!'

CHAPTER SIX

The next morning was bright and clear, and as Lottie ran along the path to school she was thinking about the evening before. She had very nearly given her mother the invitation, but then over supper her father had asked her why she didn't wear a silk or satin dress to school.

'You don't present yourself in the manner that a princess should, Lottie,' he had said. 'I'm sure your teachers wonder at you!'

Queen Mila had come to Lottie's defence, and explained that silks and satins would be most unsuitable, but that had been enough for Lottie to make up her mind.

I can't invite them. I just can't!

Wilf and Marjory were waiting for her by the gates, and she greeted them with hugs.

'Have you thought of what you're going to do for the competition?' Marjory asked.

Lottie shook her head. 'Not yet. I was wondering about choosing something so that I could disguise myself, and then Ma and Pa could come and they wouldn't recognise me. What do you think?'

Wilf grinned. 'Perhaps you could be a gargoyle!' and he did his best imitation of a dancing gargoyle as they walked along the corridor to the head teacher's study.

As they reached the door, Marjory asked, 'Are you ready to face Madam Grubeloff?'

Lottie nodded. 'I'm ready.'

But the next minute the door opened, and Aggie and Ava came marching out. Aggie stuck her nose in the air as she passed the three friends, and Lottie heard her say, 'I bet they'll never guess what we've been sorting out!'

Ava nodded. 'We'd better practise curtseying, Aggie!'

Lottie's heart sank into her boots. Had the head teacher agreed to ask her parents already? Her hand was trembling as she knocked on the door, and Madam Grubeloff called, 'Come in!'

She felt even more nervous when the head teacher smiled at her, and said, 'Lottie! What excellent timing. I was going to ask you to come and see me, and here you are – and Wilf and Marjory too. A couple of students have just suggested that we ask your parents to judge the competition. I'd intended to be the judge myself, but I can see that it would make the occasion very special. So, do tell me – can your parents come?'

Lottie swallowed. 'Ummmmm . . .' she said, wishing that the floor would open and swallow

her up. 'That is . . . I haven't quite got round to giving them the invitation yet.'

Madam Grubeloff raised her eyebrows, and there was a steely sound to her voice as she asked, 'And are you intending to give it to them?'

Lottie's mind was whirling. What should she say? There wasn't much time to think on her feet, and so she simply said, 'I'll give it to them tonight, Madam Grubeloff.'

'Good.' The head teacher was still looking stern. 'I'm not sure why you haven't given it to them already, but I imagine this is all to do with your not wanting to be recognised as a princess?'

'Yes, Madam Grubeloff. I'm sorry.'

Madam Grubeloff considered for a moment,

57

and then said, 'I really think it's time that you accepted the situation, Lottie. Give your parents the invitation tonight, and come and see me tomorrow morning with their answer.'

Marjory stepped forward. 'Please – couldn't there be a vote from the audience instead?'

Wilf nodded. 'After all, it wouldn't be very fair for Lottie's parents to be judges when she's part of the competition.'

A tiny sliver of hope sprang up in Lottie's mind as she waited for the answer. There was a pause . . . and then the head teacher stood up. 'That's a very good point, Wilf. Let me think about it.' She gave a little nod of dismissal. 'Good morning.'

Wilf, Marjory and Lottie mumbled their thanks, and headed for the door. Once outside, Lottie leaned against the wall. 'That was AWFUL!'

she said. 'Madam Grubeloff made me feel like the most horrible worm ever.'

'What do you think she'll say to you tomorrow?' Marjory asked, and Lottie sighed.

'I don't know. I'm dreading giving Ma and Pa the invitation.'

'Keep your fingers crossed,' Wilf told her. 'You never know – they might be busy.'

'They hardly ever go out anywhere,' Lottie told him gloomily.

Wilf beamed at her. 'There you are, then. If they don't like going out, they probably won't want to come!'

Marjory was looking at the clock on the wall. 'Come on . . . we'd better get to class. The bell's going to go any minute now!'

When Lottie, Wilf and Marjory walked into the classroom, they found Aggie already standing by Mrs Wilkolak's desk. 'I've finished my poem,' she announced. 'And Mrs Wilkolak says I can recite it before lessons start.' She took a deep breath.

'The story of Awesome Agatha.

In days of old, as we are told, one early summer's morn,

A truly lovely heroine called Agatha was born . . .'

The poem went on and on. Aggie's recitation was very flat and boring, and Wilf and several other students began to shift about in their seats, but Aggie kept going. The truly lovely heroine's

stepmother was mean and evil, but at last, despite every possible difficulty, Awesome Agatha triumphed. She was recognised by the world . . . and the stepmother was cast into the deepest, darkest dungeon.

As Aggie reached the end, Mrs Wilkolak nodded. 'Very well written, Aggie,' she said, 'although I think you could put more expression into the way you tell the story.'

Aggie ignored this suggestion. 'It was magnificent,' she said. 'I don't suppose anyone else will be nearly as good as me.'

'Everybody in this class is talented in one way or another, Agatha.' Mrs Wilkolak wasn't smiling any more. 'And I like my students to praise each other, not praise themselves. Now, it's time for maths. Please get out your notebooks.'

It was a struggle for Lottie to get through the rest of the day's lessons. The thought of giving her parents the invitation was a black cloud that hung over her, and it grew darker as the day went on. By the time she was on her way home, she was almost hoping a ferocious dragon would sweep down and carry her off, but no such creature appeared.

Jaws did his best to cheer her up, but even his aerial gymnastics couldn't make her smile.

Queen Mila was, as always, busy in the kitchen when Lottie came in. Not giving herself time to reconsider her decision, Lottie hurried through the door that led to the spider-infested corridors and her bedroom.

Grabbing the envelope from her bedside cabinet, she dashed back and handed it to the queen.

'What's this, dear?' her mother asked as she opened the envelope.

'It's an invitation to the school talent show,' Lottie told her. 'It's next week. Can you and Pa come?' She crossed her fingers behind her back, hoping that the answer would be no, but the queen looked pleased as she studied the card. 'I'd love to come! But it'll depend on your father. Let's see what he says.'

Lottie sat down at the table. 'Where is Pa?'

'I think he might be polishing his crown,' Queen Mila said, and as she spoke the door opened and King Lupo came in. He was frowning, and Lottie stifled a sigh.

King Lupo & Queen Mila

'Where did you get that polish from, Mila?' he demanded. 'It's worse than useless. Just look!' And he held out his crown for the queen to inspect.

'Once you've put the polish on, you have to rub it off again, dear.' Queen Mila took the crown, and gave it a quick wipe with a tea towel. 'Look! It's shining up beautifully!'

'Oh.' The king sat down with a thump. 'You didn't tell me.'

'You didn't ask, dear.' The queen put the gleaming crown back on the king's head. 'Now, how would you like to go to Lottie's school next week? We've been asked to go and watch the end-of-term talent show!'

King Lupo inspected the invitation. 'I see. And who, exactly, will be demonstrating their talents?'

'Everyone in the school,' Lottie told him.

'That sounds fun,' Queen Mila said. 'What do you think, Lupo?'

'Royalty should always support aspiring talent, especially in children,' the king announced. 'So, yes. We will attend. It will also give me the opportunity to observe how you are treated, Lottie. I have had my doubts ever since you started at Shadow Academy. From the little that you tell us, I suspect that the other pupils fail to treat you as the princess that you are. I have been seriously considering taking you out of that school, and employing a private tutor.'

'What?' Lottie went cold all over. Take her away from the wonderful Shadow Academy, and the best friends in the world? 'You can't, Pa! I LOVE school!'

The king frowned. 'I shall make my decision after this competition of yours, Lottie. If I see that you are treated in the right and appropriate fashion, then you may stay. But enough of that! Mila! What have we got for supper?'

Lottie didn't think she had ever been so miserable. She ate her supper without even noticing what it was, and escaped to her room as soon as she could.

'Oh, Jaws,' she said. 'It's going to be absolutely dreadful! Pa's going to find out that no one treats me like a princess . . . because no one knows I AM one . . . and he'll take me away! Oh, what can I do?'

CHAPTER SEVEN

Lottie's interview with Madam Grubeloff the following morning was very quick.

'So your parents are coming?' The head teacher looked pleased. 'That's splendid news! But I've come to a decision on the judging and I'm not going to ask them. I want to take up Wilf and Marjory's suggestion, and ask the audience to choose the winner.' The head teacher gave Lottie a questioning look. 'I was thinking, though, that I would ask your parents if they'd be kind enough to present the trophy. You wouldn't mind, would you?'

Lottie did her best to smile, and curtseyed. 'Of course not, Madam Grubeloff.'

The classroom was buzzing as Lottie walked in. Mrs Wilkolak was writing a list of the different acts on the blackboard, and there was applause for each one. As Lottie sat down, Mrs Wilkolak asked, 'Ah! Lottie! Have you decided what you're doing?'

Lottie blinked. She had been so unhappy the night before at the possibility of being taken away from her friends that she hadn't really had a chance to think of anything else. She seized on the first idea that came to her.

'I . . . I'm going to sing the Forest Song . . . the one we sing at the Evening Howl sometimes.'

'Excellent.' Mrs Wilkolak looked at the board, and smiled. 'So that's everybody. What a

wonderful evening it's going to be! Now, practise all you can this weekend, because on Monday you'll be rehearsing in the Great Hall – don't forget to bring any props you might need. And, if you want to bring your costumes to wear on Monday, please do – but it's fine to wait until Tuesday if that's easier. Is that all clear? Are there any questions?'

Aggie put up her hand. 'Please – has Madam Grubeloff asked the king and queen to come?'

Mrs Wilkolak raised her eyebrows. 'I'd prefer for you not to worry about things like that, Aggie. It's much more important that your mothers and fathers and carers and grandparents enjoy themselves.'

As soon as the bell rang for break, Wilf and Marjory pounced on Lottie. 'Lottie! What is it? You look so unhappy! Was Madam Grubeloff very cross with you?'

Lottie, fighting back tears, shook her head. 'It's much, MUCH worse than that. Pa's threatening to take me away from Shadow Academy.'

Her friends stared at her. 'Why? What have you done?'

'Nothing,' Lottie said miserably. 'It's just this stupid royal thing. Ma and Pa are coming next Tuesday, and Pa wants to see everyone bowing and scraping to me and calling me Princess Lottie. He says that if I'm not being treated like a princess he'll keep me at home with a tutor.'

'WOWSERS! That's . . . I don't know what to say. That's . . . that's just the most terrible thing ever.' Wilf was so upset that he could hardly speak.

Marjory hugged Lottie hard. 'We'll think of something!' she promised. 'We absolutely HAVE to have you here! Oh, Lottie . . .' and she hugged Lottie again.

'So, what's the amazing Lottie Luna done now?' Aggie was strolling past, arm in arm with Ava. 'Having second thoughts about singing a stupid school song?'

'Lottie's song's going to be the best thing in the show!' Wilf scowled at Aggie. 'Come on, Lottie. We've got better things to do than talk to people who think they're smarter than everyone else.' And he, Lottie and Marjory hurried away down the corridor.

'Thank you,' Lottie said, and she took a deep breath as they reached the playground. 'I can't

bear to think about it any more. It's too awful . . . and I really, really, REALLY want to make the most of school while I'm still here. Could we just pretend that everything's all right?'

Marjory and Wilf nodded. 'We'll try.'

Much to Lottie's surprise, her mother was waiting for her at the castle door when she reached home that evening.

'Lottie!' Queen Mila was glowing with excitement. 'You'll never guess what's happened!'

Lottie swallowed. She had a sinking feeling that she did know, but she shook her head.

'Your father and I have been invited to present the trophy at your school competition!'

Doing her best to sound enthusiastic, Lottie said, 'Oh! Ummmm . . . good.'

'So,' the queen went on, 'I was thinking you ought to have something special to wear because you're our daughter. I went to have a look in those chests where we found the top hat – I remembered I'd noticed some dresses there – and I've found the perfect outfit for you! Come and see!'

Wondering what her mother might consider perfect, Lottie followed her along the

corridor. The portraits of her ancestors looked
even more depressed than usual, and she made
a face at a particularly gloomy-looking girl in
a hideous green ballgown. Her mother saw
where she was looking, and gave a little shriek of
delight.

'Lottie! That's it! That's the dress I've chosen
for you! And that pretty girl is your . . . what
would she be now? A great-great-aunt perhaps?'
Queen Mila peered at the nameplate under the

KING VLAD

Queen Scylla

picture. 'Princess Valottina, musical to the end. How lovely!'

Lottie stared at her mother. 'Ma! You don't expect me to wear that, do you? It's ghastly!'

'Nonsense, Lottie!' Her mother took her arm, and hurried her into the kitchen. Hanging on a cupboard was the green ballgown, and it looked even worse than it had in the portrait. Queen Mila beamed at Lottie.

'Go and try it on, dear. Your father thinks it's perfect!'

Lottie took the ballgown, and trailed to her room. Not only was everyone going to find out that she was a princess, but they'd also see her dressed in the most horribly princessy garment she'd ever seen.

She had just slipped the dress over her head,

and was staring at her
almost unrecognisable
self in the mirror,
when her mother
came bustling in.
'There! It's a perfect
fit!' She stepped
back, and inspected her
drooping daughter. 'Dear
Lottie . . . do try to smile! Now, I just came to say
that your father has decided that he and I will
travel to the competition in the weremobile . . .
Will you be able to come with us?'

'I'll be at school, Ma,' Lottie said. 'We've got a
run-through on Tuesday afternoon.'

'Oh, of course.' The queen nodded. 'Well – at
least we'll be able to come home together.' She

gave the ballgown a considering look. 'I really believe that you'll be the belle of the ball!'

Lottie was too depressed to argue. She thanked her mother and then, as soon as the queen had left, put her usual clothes back on.

I *don't think things could possibly get any worse*, she thought, and she looked at her moonstone necklace. Just as she had expected, it was dull and colourless. *That's exactly how I feel.*

CHAPTER EIGHT

On Monday morning, as Lottie hurried through the school gates, she saw Wilf and Marjory carrying a large box between them.

'We've got Hopper,' Wilf said cheerfully.

Lottie peered inside at the white rabbit who waggled his little pink nose back at her.

'We thought we ought to rehearse with him today,' Marjory told her.

As always, Lottie felt better when she saw her friends, and the three of them walked into school together.

Mrs Wilkolak was standing in the main hall, holding a list. When she saw Wilf and Marjory, she waved at them. 'I've put you two first in the programme,' she said. 'I thought your rabbit might be better behaved if he's not in his box for too long.'

'Thanks,' Wilf said. 'Lottie's going to look after him until he's needed, so he should be okay.'

'That sounds sensible.' Mrs Wilkolak consulted her papers. 'You're at the end of the programme, Lottie. I'd like you to be last, if you don't mind. I think the Forest Song will be a bit of a show-

88

stopper! Did you know it used to be the royal anthem? King Lupo will be thrilled.'

Lottie opened her mouth to say that her father couldn't tell the difference between one tune and another, but luckily she was interrupted.

Aggie and Ava had come into the hall behind her, and Aggie's eyes sharpened as she listened. Pushing forward, she asked, 'The royal anthem?'

'That's right.' Mrs Wilkolak nodded. 'And I expect you want to know when you're on, Aggie. I've put you just before Lottie. That will make such an excellent finale . . . first your poem, then Lottie with the Forest Song, and that wonderful chorus. Perhaps the king might even join in!'

Aggie didn't make any comment, but there was a thoughtful look on her face as she walked away.

Lottie's classroom was hardly
recognisable when she came in.
Two boys were juggling, three

girls were doing

handstands,

Aggie was reciting

with her hand on her

heart, Ava was playing the

trumpet – the noise

was incredible – until Mrs Wilkolak
came through the door and held
up her hand for silence.

'Good morning, class!

I have some news for

you. Madam Grubeloff has asked

me to tell you that the competition

will be judged by the audience.'

'Oh . . . BOTHER!'

Lottie heard Aggie's exclamation very clearly, but Mrs Wilkolak didn't seem to notice. 'So, the audience will vote . . . but – and this is very exciting! – the giant gargoyle will be presented to the winner by none other than King Lupo and Queen Mila!'

There was a delighted gasp from Aggie, and Ava gave a loud whoop. Looking round, Lottie saw that everyone was smiling, and she squashed a sigh.

'In a moment or two we'll be going to the Great Hall,' the teacher went on. 'Madam Grubeloff will be watching, so make sure you do your best.'

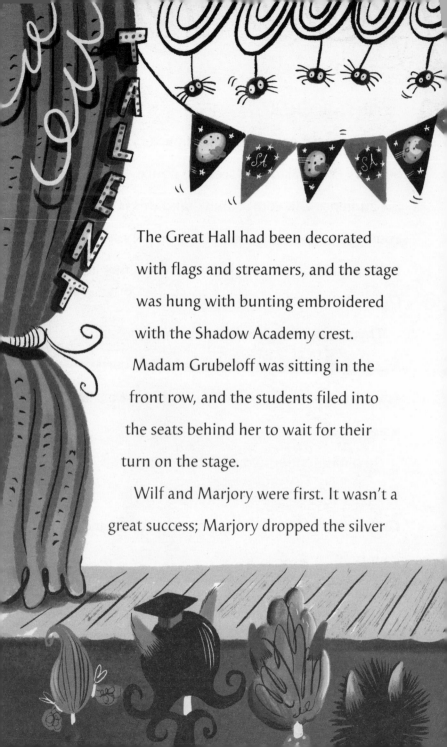

The Great Hall had been decorated
with flags and streamers, and the stage
was hung with bunting embroidered
with the Shadow Academy crest.
Madam Grubeloff was sitting in the
front row, and the students filed into
the seats behind her to wait for their
turn on the stage.

Wilf and Marjory were first. It wasn't a
great success; Marjory dropped the silver

rings twice, and Wilf forgot his
best card trick.

'I knew it'd be rubbish,' Aggie whispered to Ava, and Madam Grubeloff turned round with a frown.

'Try to be supportive, Aggie!'

Lottie crossed her fingers and hoped that nothing else would go wrong. She stood guard over Hopper and waited for the moment when Wilf pretended his top hat had fallen off by mistake. As the hat rolled to the side of the stage, she popped the rabbit inside, together with a carrot. Wilf picked up the hat, and Marjory tapped it with her wand.

'Abracadabra!' At once Hopper sat bolt upright, his white ears wiggling, and the carrot in his mouth, and Lottie breathed a sigh of relief.

'Well done, Wilf and Marjory,' Madam Grubeloff said. 'That was excellent!'

Next to perform were a group of dancers, followed by Ava playing the trumpet. Jugglers, acrobats and stand-up comics all had their turn, and Lottie began to feel more and more nervous.

CHAPTER NINE

It was after lunch before Madam Grubeloff
called Aggie and Lottie's names.

Aggie went first. She pranced on to the stage
and began her poem – but she hadn't got very far
when Madam Grubeloff stopped her.

'Aggie, it sounds a little bit flat. Could you put
more expression into it, do you think?'

Aggie looked so furious that for a moment
Lottie thought she was going to answer back.
Instead, she swallowed hard and said, 'Yes,
Madam Grubeloff.'

The poem went on, and Madam Grubeloff interrupted three more times to ask Aggie to repeat a verse. At the end she said, 'I congratulate you on your excellent poem, Agatha – but do try not to mumble. We want the audience to enjoy it!'

As Aggie glowered, Lottie climbed on to the stage to sing her song. She was nervous, but her voice was clear and true, and at the end Madam Grubeloff clapped loudly. 'Well done! That'll have the whole audience on their feet! And Aggie – did

you notice how Lottie made sure we could hear every word? And how she looked out into the audience in order to include them? Try to do the same with your poem, please. We want everyone to have a lovely evening.'

As Aggie, quivering with fury, stamped towards her seat, Madam Grubeloff made her way on to the stage. 'Thank you, everyone! Only one act can be the actual winner of the giant gargoyle, but every single one of you will be a winner in my eyes. I really appreciate the effort you've all made, and by way of a thank-you I've arranged a little

after-show party for tomorrow . . . and you're all invited.'

'Wow!' Marjory's eyes were shining as she, Lottie and Wilf collected their things and headed back to the classroom. 'A party! That'll be so much fun! Will your parents let you stay for it, Lottie?'

Lottie sighed. 'I expect so . . . but I might not want to come.'

'Why not?' Wilf asked in surprise.

'Everyone will know I'm a princess by then . . . and I'm scared Pa will do something terrible like announce that I'm leaving the school.' Lottie stifled a sob. 'And, on top of everything else, I'm going to look dreadful. Ma's found this absolutely ghastly ballgown that belonged to some ancient ancestor of mine, and I've got to wear it. It's the most princessy dress you ever saw, and I absolutely HATE it! Oh, Wilf . . . Marjory . . . what am I going to do?' And a tear rolled down her cheek.

Wilf and Marjory looked at her, and then at each other. Lottie was their best friend and she needed help. Wilf rubbed his ear while he tried to think of something helpful to say. 'Erm . . . what kind of ancestor was she?'

'She was called Princess Valottina,' Lottie told him, 'and she liked music. She looks totally miserable in her picture. I bet she hated the dress just as much as I do.'

'It's a pretty name, though,' Marjory said. 'Valottina. It's a bit like Lottie.'

Wilf made a sudden strange noise, and Lottie and Marjory looked at him in alarm. 'Brain in gear!' He waved his arms. 'Wait for it . . . wait for

it . . . Wilf's thinking . . . YESSSS!' And he leaped in the air. 'THAT'S IT!'

Lottie stared at him. 'What is?'

'The answer!' Wilf did a triumphant backflip, and came up beaming. 'Lottie . . . for the talent show, you have to play the part of your ancestor! You'll be Princess Valottina – Lottie for short! Marjory and I'll make sure we call you that every time your ma or pa are nearby, and we'll bow and curtsey and all that sort of thing – and we'll tell everyone else to call you Princess Lottie as well! So, if Aggie – or any of her beastly friends – hears you being called Princess Lottie, they'll just think it's part of your act. And what's more –' Wilf looked as if he was about to explode with delight – 'your pa will think we're doing it for real!'

There was a very long pause . . . and then

Marjory gave a whoop of triumph. 'Wilf! You're a super-brilliant mega-genius!'

Wilf grinned. 'I know. But actually I wouldn't have thought of it if you hadn't said that about Valottina sounding like Lottie.'

Lottie wiped her eyes. 'Do you really think it might work?' she asked, and her friends nodded so enthusiastically that she hugged them both.

By the time Lottie had walked home, she had had enough time to think of all the things that could go wrong with Wilf's plan. All the same, she still felt as if there was a tiny glimmer of hope, and she was able to smile at her mother as she came through the door.

Queen Mila greeted her with a kiss. 'All ready

for tomorrow?' she asked. 'I'm so looking forward to the show! Now, remind me of the instructions.'

'I need to take my dress with me when I go to school,' Lottie told her. 'I think morning lessons are normal, but then we've got a run-through in the afternoon, and I'll stay on until the talent show. I'll see you there, Ma! Oh, and Madam Grubeloff has arranged an after-show party for us, so I won't be able to come home with you.'

Her mother nodded. 'That's fine. Your father says we must leave as soon as we've presented the prize.' She sighed, and added, 'I'd have loved to stay and meet all your friends, but your father wants to retain an air of royal mystery!'

CHAPTER TEN

Tuesday, the day of the Shadow Academy
talent competition, was grey and cloudy. Lottie,
so anxious that her stomach felt as if it was full of
butterflies, packed the green ballgown carefully,
and kissed her parents goodbye.

'I'll see you later,' she said, 'and I hope you like
the show.' And then she was off.

Shadow Academy was unusually busy when
Lottie came hurrying through the main door.

Students were rushing about in all directions.
Aggie was hauling a suitcase across
the floor, Ava was checking
the contents of her trumpet
case, and Marjory was
waiting for Lottie. She was
clutching her and Wilf's outfits,
and she greeted her friend with a beaming smile.

'Wilf's gone to put Hopper in the caretaker's
garden,' she said, 'and we've got to hang our
costumes in the library. I'm longing to see your
dress, Princess Lottie!'

'Princess Lottie?' Aggie had overheard
Marjory, and her eyes narrowed. 'What do you
mean, Princess Lottie?'

'Didn't you know?' Marjory asked. 'Lottie's
going to be playing the part of an old-fashioned

princess called Princess Valottina.' She turned to Lottie, and gave her the tiniest wink. 'Isn't that right, Princess Lottie?'

'Yes! She's—' Lottie remembered just in time that she couldn't explain that Valottina was an ancestor of hers. 'She's in the history books. And she liked music, so I thought she'd be just right for my song.'

'Oh.' Aggie didn't ask any more questions, but she followed Lottie and Marjory to the library. When Lottie pulled the green ballgown out of the bag, Marjory gave a squeak of excitement.

'It's AMAZING! It's just right for a princess from the olden days!'

Ava came to see what they were doing. 'Where did you get it?'

'My mum found it somewhere,' Lottie said truthfully, and Ava wrinkled her nose.

'It smells of mothballs! I bet she found it in someone's charity box. Yuck! I wouldn't want to wear that, would you, Aggie?'

Aggie was studying the ballgown, with all its ruffles and sequins and hooped skirts, and there was a curious expression on her face. 'No,' she said, but she didn't sound very convinced. 'It's much too fussy. Come on, Ava. Let's get our dresses hung up.'

When Lottie and Marjory reached their classroom, they found that Mrs Wilkolak was handing out a general-knowledge test.

'You're all going to have a very exciting afternoon and evening,' the teacher said, 'so I want to see you concentrating this morning. You can work in twos or threes – but don't talk too loudly!'

99

As always, Lottie and Marjory settled down with Wilf and, by the time the test had been completed and marked, the lunch bell had rung.

'Goodness!' Marjory said. 'Didn't the morning go quickly?'

'And it's the run-through after lunch,' Wilf said. 'No more lessons today!'

Lottie nodded. 'Are we meant to be wearing our costumes this afternoon?'

Mrs Wilkolak heard her. 'Wait until the evening, Lottie. The run-through is just to check that everyone knows the order of events. I'd like you to get on the stage, announce the name of your act, and then leave again.'

'Lottie's got the most wonderful dress for tonight, Mrs Wilkolak,' Marjory said. 'She's going to look just like a real princess!'

108

Lottie made a face. 'I think it's hideous – but it is very princessy.'

'I look forward to seeing it,' Mrs Wilkolak told her. 'Now, hurry up, or you'll be late for lunch!'

Mrs Wilkolak was in charge of the run-through, and she greeted Wilf, Lottie and Marjory with a smile. 'Are you ready? You're on first.' She raised her eyebrows at Wilf. 'I hope you haven't got your rabbit with you!'

Wilf grinned. 'No, Mrs Wilkolak. He's in the caretaker's garden.'

'I'm glad to hear it,' the teacher said. 'Now – let's begin!'

101

The run-through went almost too smoothly.
Only two acts got the order wrong, and they
were quickly sorted out. By the time Aggie had
announced the title of her story, Mrs Wilkolak
was looking relieved and pleased.

'Can't I recite my poem?' Aggie asked. 'I'm sure
everyone would like to hear it again.'

Mrs Wilkolak shook her head. 'I'm afraid it's
too long, Aggie. Save your energies for tonight.'
She glanced up at the stage where Lottie was
waiting. 'Why don't we ask Lottie to sing her song
instead? You wouldn't mind, would you, Princess
Lottie?'

Lottie shook her head, and began to sing. Her
voice soared up into the rafters, and the students
in the hall held their breath as they listened.

102

'When the dark night sky is pierced with stars

And the wind whispers secrets to the trees

And the moon rides high like a sailing ship

That sails over cloudy seas . . .

That's when the werewolves howl their howl

That's when the werewolves howl their howl

That's when the werewolves howl their howl

So howl, howl, howl with me!'

As soon as Lottie came to the chorus, every single student and teacher in the hall joined in with such enthusiasm that Madam Grubeloff came hurrying out of her study to see what was happening.

'The old royal anthem!' she said as the final howl died away. 'That's going to be wonderful! King Lupo and Queen Mila will be absolutely thrilled!' And she gave Lottie the tiniest of winks before she left the stage.

CHAPTER ELEVEN

Lottie, blushing furiously, jumped down the steps. As she made her way to join Wilf and Marjory, several of the other students patted her on the back and said, 'Well done, Princess Lottie!'

'See?' Wilf was jubilant. 'It's going to work! Everyone's calling you Princess Lottie!'

'And your song was wonderful!' Marjory beamed at her friend. 'Your parents will absolutely love it!'

Still conscious of the butterflies in her stomach, which seemed to be getting worse by the minute, Lottie made a face. 'Fingers crossed. What's happening now?'

'Mrs Wilkolak said there are snacks waiting for us in the classroom,' Marjory said. 'And then we're supposed to read a book quietly so we have a rest before the competition. There won't be an Evening Howl tonight – we'll be getting ready instead, because the audience arrives at half past five!'

To Lottie's anxious mind, the minutes flew. Every time she looked at the clock, it was nearer the moment when her parents would arrive and, when Mrs Wilkolak stood up from her desk to say it was time to get ready, her stomach lurched.

'I'd better go and collect Hopper,' Wilf said.

'I'll see you in a couple of minutes!'

Lottie took a deep breath. *I've got to be brave!* she told herself, and she and Marjory hurried to the library to find their costumes.

Aggie was already there, dressed in a very expensive-looking dress covered in frills and little silver bows, and she sneered as Lottie picked up her ballgown. 'I hope your ancient old dress doesn't fall to bits, Lottie! And don't think I'm going to call you Princess Lottie, because I'm not. You're the very last person on earth I'd think of as a princess, so there!'

Lottie shrugged. 'That's okay,' she said, and she turned her back on Aggie. As she did so, she saw Marjory winking at her, and she had to dive inside her dress to stop herself from laughing.

'What are you sniggering at?' Aggie asked angrily. 'I saw you!'

'It was nothing,' Marjory said quickly. 'Just me and Lottie being silly.'

Aggie stuck her nose in the air. 'That's exactly what you are!'

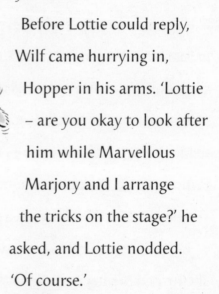

Before Lottie could reply, Wilf came hurrying in, Hopper in his arms. 'Lottie – are you okay to look after him while Marvellous Marjory and I arrange the tricks on the stage?' he asked, and Lottie nodded. 'Of course.'

Five minutes later, Lottie, stroking Hopper's ears, heard the voices of the audience as they began

to arrive. They sounded very excited; Lottie felt a wave of sadness sweep over her as she realised she might never be part of the school again if Wilf's plan didn't work. For a moment, she felt like crying, but then she shook herself. *It's going to be okay*, she thought. *It HAS to be!*

'Princess Lottie!' Mrs Wilkolak had come bustling into the library. 'We need you to be at the side of the stage before the curtain goes up. Wilf and Marjory are waiting for you, and the audience is almost settled.'

Aggie came hurrying from the other end of the room. 'Mrs Wilkolak! Have the king and queen come yet?'

'They've arrived, and they're being welcomed by Madam Grubeloff in her study,' Mrs Wilkolak told her. 'They'll take their seats at the last moment.'

'Oooooh!' Aggie clasped her hands together. 'I can't wait to meet them!' And she gave a twirl, holding out her skirts.

TINGALINGALING!

'Quick!' Mrs Wilkolak gave Lottie a push. 'That's the signal that the king and queen are sitting down! Get on to the stage as fast as you can!'

Clutching Hopper, Lottie did as she was told. Wilf and Marjory were already standing behind the closed curtains, and Lottie blew them a kiss as she and Hopper hid themselves at the side of the stage.

'Good luck!' she whispered, and then they heard Madam Grubeloff's voice from the other side of the curtains.

110

'The Shadow Academy welcomes you all,' she said, 'and may I offer an especially warm welcome to King Lupo and Queen Mila, who have most graciously agreed to present the trophy to our winner this evening.'

There was a ripple of applause, and Lottie felt a sudden warm glow. *They like Ma and Pa!*

But Madam Grubeloff was still talking. 'And now I'd like to introduce our very first act. Please put your hands together for the Two Incredibles!'

There was a smattering of applause, the curtains swept apart and the competition began. Wilf and Marjory bowed and curtseyed, and Wilf brought out his handful of cards.

'Dear audience,' he said, 'please watch VERY carefully!' and there was a murmur of excitement as he and Marjory went through their tricks.

111

It seemed only seconds before the act was nearly over, and Wilf tossed his top hat towards Lottie. She tucked Hopper and a carrot inside, and Wilf swooped down and picked the hat up. Marjory tapped it with the wand – and Hopper popped up exactly as he was meant to do. The curtains closed to a roar of appreciation, and Wilf and Marjory hurriedly tidied their props away before disappearing down the steps at the other side of the stage, Hopper tucked under Wilf's arm.

The acts followed one after another and, although there was plenty of clapping and laughter, Lottie was sure that Wilf and Marjory had been the most popular so far.

I do hope they win, she thought. *It would be so lovely if they did!*

At last it was Aggie's turn. She arranged herself carefully at the front of the stage, and before Madam Grubeloff could introduce her she sank into a low curtsey. 'Your Majesties,' she said, 'allow me to introduce myself. I am Agatha Claws.'

There was a loud cheer from the front row. 'Come on, our Aggie!'

Aggie beamed, and held out her arms in an overly dramatic gesture. 'Tonight, Your Majesties,' she announced, 'I'm going to do something you'll absolutely love,' and she gave a self-conscious little giggle. 'Please join in, and we'll have lots of fun. I've heard that this is one of your favourites, so it's especially for you!' And, as Lottie's eyes

113

opened wide in shock and horror,

Aggie began to sing the Forest Song.

CHAPTER TWELVE

As Aggie sang, so fast that nobody could hear the words, and very out of tune, Lottie's mind was whirling. What should she do? She couldn't possibly sing the same song now . . . but she couldn't walk on to the stage and do nothing either. She clenched her fists, and shut her eyes. *Think, Lottie! Think!*

Aggie was now reaching the chorus, and was obviously expecting everyone to join in. She marched round and round the stage, waving her arms like a windmill, but even though she sang louder and louder hers was the only voice. In a last desperate attempt, she stopped, and shouted, 'Come ON, everyone! Howl, howl, HOWL!'

But first there was dead silence . . . and then this silence was followed by an enormous burst of laughter.

Lottie, peeping round the side of the stage, saw Aggie's face turn first scarlet with embarrassment, then pale, and then scarlet again and, to her surprise, she found herself thinking, *Poor, POOR Aggie!*

All Aggie could do was finish the song. She rushed off the stage, the curtains closed, and Madam Grubeloff came hurrying up the steps.

'Lottie! Whatever happened? You were going to sing the Forest Song!'

Lottie nodded. 'Yes, Madam Grubeloff.' And, as she spoke, an idea popped into her head. Before she had time to change her mind, she said, 'Aggie and I . . . we . . . we swapped. I'm going to recite her poem, in my character of Princess Valottina.'

'You are?' Madam Grubeloff stared at Lottie, but before Lottie could answer the curtains swept open again – and the head teacher had no choice but to introduce the final act.

'Last, but by no means least, we have our very own Princess Lottie.'

Lottie walked to the centre of the stage, her knees trembling. She could see her parents sitting on small raised platform at the back of the Great Hall, and her mother gave her a little wave.

'I'm here to tell you the story of Awesome

Agatha,' Lottie announced, and she heard a faint

murmur from the students in the audience.

Crossing her fingers behind her back, and hoping

that her remarkable memory wouldn't let her

down, Lottie began.

'In days of old, as we are told, one early

summer's morn . . .'

She told the story as well as she could, and

as she went on she realised the audience was

listening intently. When she reached the climax, and Agatha's wicked stepmother's treachery was discovered, there was a loud gasp . . . and as the heroine finally triumphed there was a shout of HURRAH! and the audience leaped to their feet, cheering wildly. The applause went on and on, and Lottie, blushing furiously, curtseyed over and over again until Madam Grubeloff came sweeping on to the stage and held up her hand for silence.

'Thank you, Princess Lottie. A truly wonderful story, excellently well told.'

For a fraction of a second Lottie hesitated, but then the memory of Aggie's agonised face flashed into her mind, and she turned to the audience.

'This poem was written by –' she took a breath – 'my very clever friend, Agatha Claws.'

Madam Grubeloff looked at Lottie. 'That's very

generous of you, Princess Lottie,' she said, and she gave her a beaming smile. 'Perhaps we should ask Agatha to come up on the stage, so we can congratulate her too.'

'Yes, please,' Lottie said.

There was a pause before Aggie slowly came to join them. Her eyes were very red as if she had been crying, and she didn't look at Lottie as she curtseyed to the head teacher. 'Thank you,' she said. She shuffled her feet, and stared at the ground as the audience clapped. As they finished, she gave Lottie a sideways look. Then, with an obvious effort, she said, 'Thank you, Lottie.' She swallowed hard, and added, 'I mean . . . Princess Lottie.'

Madam Grubeloff had moved to the front of the stage. 'We want you, the audience, to decide who is the winner of our talent show. If you agree with me that there is a very obvious winner, would you please stand?'

The entire audience rose to its feet, and as it did so Wilf called out, 'Hurrah for Princess Lottie Luna!'

'Wilf – you've taken the words from my mouth,' the head teacher said, but she didn't sound angry. She turned to Lottie, and shook her hand. 'Congratulations, Princess Lottie. Please make your way to King Lupo and Queen Mila . . . and receive your well-deserved prize – the giant gargoyle!'

As King Lupo picked up the giant gargoyle to present it to Lottie, everyone gasped. The silver

gleamed under the lights, and as Lottie looked at it she was almost sure that the strange face winked at her. 'I hereby present you with your prize,' King Lupo said, as Lottie took the trophy in her arms.

'Thank you, Your Majesty,' she said.

Her father beamed at her. 'I'm delighted, Lottie! Delighted! It seems that the entire school are treating you exactly as I would wish. Shadow Academy is the perfect school for you!'

Lottie curtseyed very low. 'Thank you,' she said, and there were stars in her eyes as her father

gathered his royal robes around him and stood up.

'Come, Mila! Our duty is done!' And, with a regal wave, the king marched out of the Great Hall. The queen stayed just long enough to kiss Lottie. 'Well done, dear,' she said. 'That was wonderful!' And then she too was gone, and Lottie was free to dance her way to join Wilf and Marjory, the silver giant gargoyle in her arms.

It took Lottie far longer than usual to reach the dining hall. So many of her friends wanted to congratulate her, and look at the giant gargoyle, that she had to keep stopping. By the time she got through the door, the after-show party was in full swing, and she paused for a moment to enjoy the sight.

This is my school, and these are my friends, she told herself, *and it's – it's SO WONDERFUL!*

Wilf saw her, and came rushing over. 'Well done, Lottie!' he said. 'Marjory and I nearly died when Aggie sang your song! It was so clever of you to remember her poem – and you actually made it sound brilliant!'

Lottie shook her head. 'I was scared I'd forget some of it . . . it was just luck that I didn't.'

'It was your amazing memory!' Marjory had come to join Wilf. 'Aggie's gone home, but she asked me to give you this,' and she handed Lottie a piece of paper.

'What is it?' Lottie unfolded the paper.

DEAR LOTTIE,

THANK YOU FOR READING MY POEM. I'M VERY SORRY THAT I TRIED TO SING YOUR SONG. I WANTED THE KING AND QUEEN TO LIKE ME THE BEST, AND MADAM GRUBELOFF SAID IT WAS THEIR FAVOURITE SONG SO THAT'S WHY I SANG IT. BUT THEY DIDN'T LIKE IT. I SAW THE KING FROWNING DREADFULLY.

I WON'T BE BACK AT SCHOOL TOMORROW. MADAM GRUBELOFF IS VERY CROSS WITH ME. I KNOW YOU'RE NOT A REAL PRINCESS, BUT YOU BEHAVED LIKE ONE BECAUSE YOU WERE NICE TO ME WHEN I WAS MEAN TO YOU.

I HOPE WE CAN BE FRIENDS.

LOVE FROM

AGGIE X

'Wow!' Marjory's eyes were like saucers. 'What are you going to say to her?'

Lottie smiled. 'Just at the moment I want to be friends with everyone forever!'

'Okay. Just as long as you're our best friend!' Wilf said, and the three of them linked arms, and went to join the party.

Chapter Thirteen

The dining room was buzzing as Lottie finally walked in, the giant gargoyle in her arms. She put it on the end of the table and patted its head . . . and, once again, it winked cheerfully at her.

'Did you see that?' she asked Marjory. 'It winked at me!'

Marjory laughed. 'It's telling you it's pleased you won. Lottie – just look at that cake!'

Lottie looked . . .

and gasped. In among the plates of sandwiches oozing with delicious fillings, jars of crunchy chocolate biscuits, slices of bubbling cheesy pizza, and bowls of glistening fruit, was the most enormous cake . . . and it was in the shape of a building.

'It's Shadow Academy!' she said, and she was right. The cake was covered in little silver moons and stars, and as Lottie looked closer she saw that there were tiny faces at every window . . . the faces of all the students.

'It's AMAZING!' she breathed.

'I think you should cut the first slice, Princess Lottie.' It was Madam Grubeloff, and she gave Lottie a warm smile.

Marjory clapped her hands. 'Please, Madam

Grubeloff – could we have a countdown?'

'YES!' There was a universal cheer, and the countdown began.

'Five . . . four . . . three . . . two . . . ONE!'

As Lottie plunged the knife into the cake, Wilf shouted, 'Three cheers for Princess Lottie!'

'HURRAH for Princess Lottie!' The shout echoed round the room.

Wilf was grinning from ear to ear as Lottie handed him the first slice.

'Our plan worked, didn't it?' he said proudly, and Lottie hugged him . . . and then she hugged Marjory too.

'It was wonderful,' she agreed. 'Pa said this is the perfect school for me!' She gave a little skip of happiness. 'And he was quite right . . . because I have the most PERFECT friends!'

Later that evening, Lottie walked slowly home, thinking happily about her day. Jaws was on her shoulder, and her moonstone necklace was shining so brightly that it looked like a star. The giant silver gargoyle was tucked under her arm, and she was singing softly to herself.

'When the dark night sky is pierced with stars
And the wind whispers secrets to the trees
And the moon rides high like a sailing ship
That sails over cloudy seas . . .
That's when the werewolves howl their howl
So howl, howl, howl with me
For nobody, nobody, nobody at all
Is quite as happy as me!'

HAVE YOU READ LOTTIE LUNA'S OTHER ADVENTURES?

BOOK ONE

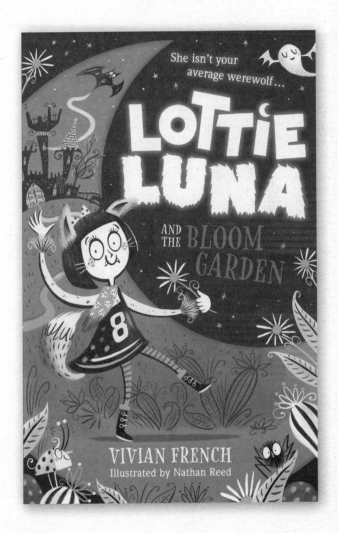

She isn't your average werewolf...

LOTTIE LUNA
AND THE BLOOM GARDEN

VIVIAN FRENCH
Illustrated by Nathan Reed

BOOK TWO

She isn't your average werewolf...

LOTTIE LUNA

AND THE TWILIGHT PARTY

VIVIAN FRENCH

Illustrated by Nathan Reed

BOOK THREE

She isn't your average werewolf...

LOTTIE LUNA
and the FANG FAIRY

VIVIAN FRENCH
Illustrated by Nathan Reed